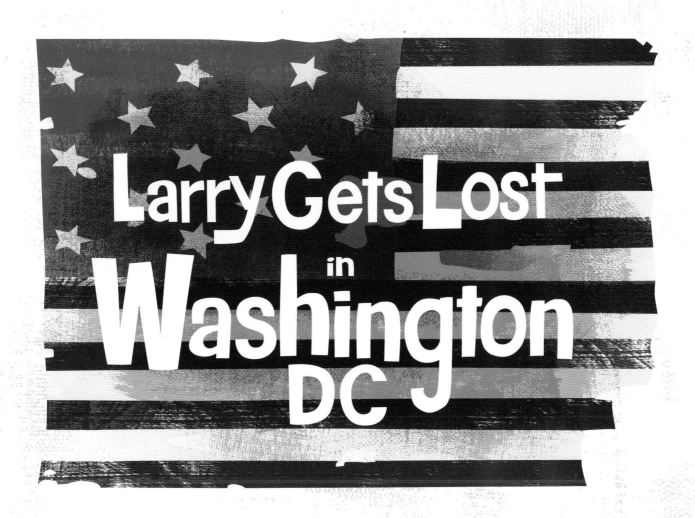

Larry Gets Lost in Washington DC

Illustrated by John Skewes
Written by John Skewes and Andrew Fox

little bigfoot
an imprint of sasquatch books
seattle, wa

Dedicated to Captain T. J. Skewes Jr., USN
Commander of the USS *Crowley*, Pacific Theater, WWII

Manufactured in China by C&C Offset Printing Co. Ltd. Shanghai,
in January 2014

Published by Little Bigfoot, an imprint of Sasquatch Books
20 19 18 17 16 15 14   9 8 7 6 5 4 3 2 1

Editor: Susan Roxborough
Project editor: Michelle Hope Anderson
Illustrations: John Skewes
Book design: Mint Design
Interior composition: Sarah Plein

Library of Congress Cataloging-in-Publication Data is available.

ISBN: 978-1-57061-899-4

Sasquatch Books
1904 Third Avenue, Suite 710
Seattle, WA 98101
(206) 467-4300
www.sasquatchbooks.com
custserv@sasquatchbooks.com

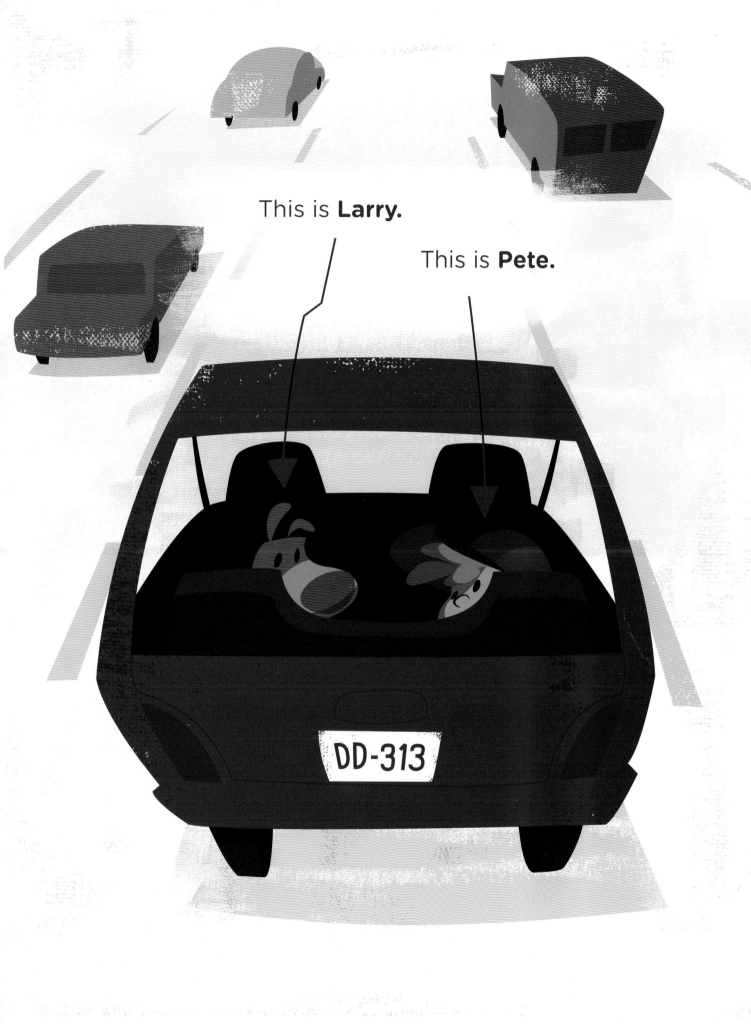

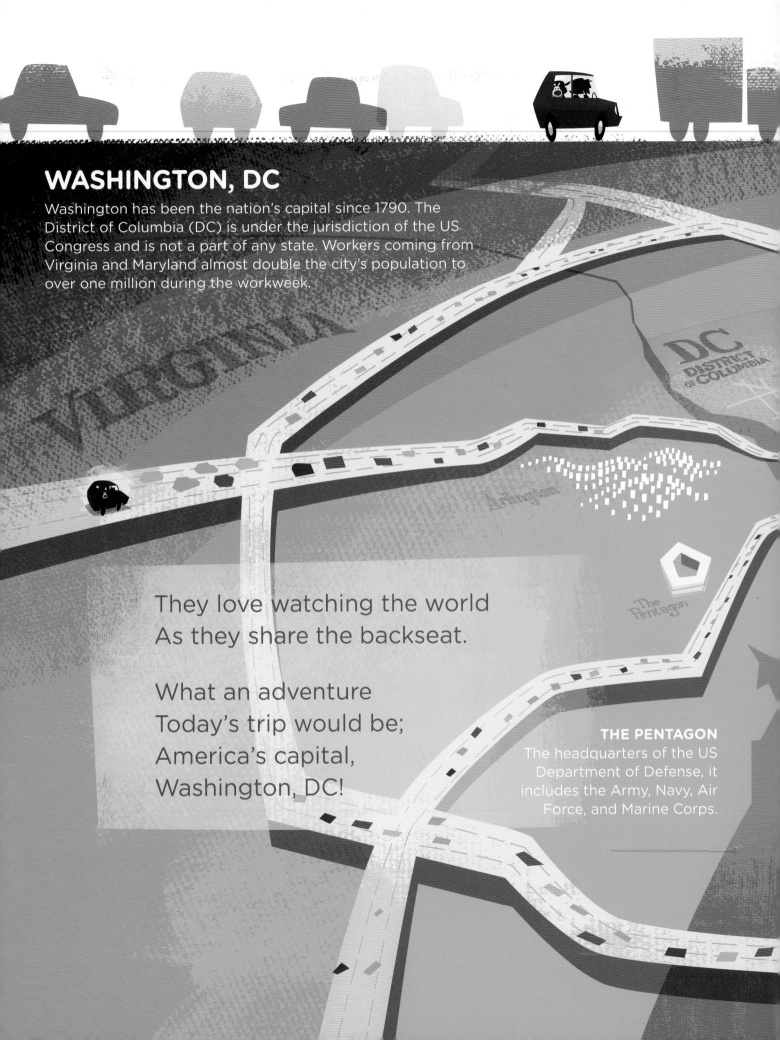

WASHINGTON, DC

Washington has been the nation's capital since 1790. The District of Columbia (DC) is under the jurisdiction of the US Congress and is not a part of any state. Workers coming from Virginia and Maryland almost double the city's population to over one million during the workweek.

They love watching the world
As they share the backseat.

What an adventure
Today's trip would be;
America's capital,
Washington, DC!

THE PENTAGON
The headquarters of the US Department of Defense, it includes the Army, Navy, Air Force, and Marine Corps.

THE BELTWAY

Interstate 495 is a 64-mile highway that circles Washington, DC, and passes through Virginia and Maryland.

They rolled down the freeway,
A big "belt," they say,
Filled with folks who work hard
For the nation each day.

They stopped for a moment
Where stones painted white
Stood proud, still, and silent
Like stars in the night.

ARLINGTON NATIONAL CEMETERY
Established in 1864, Arlington is a 624-acre military cemetery and the resting place of veterans from every conflict beginning with the American Civil War.

So much to see here,
And so much to learn,
But now Larry's stomach
Was starting to churn.

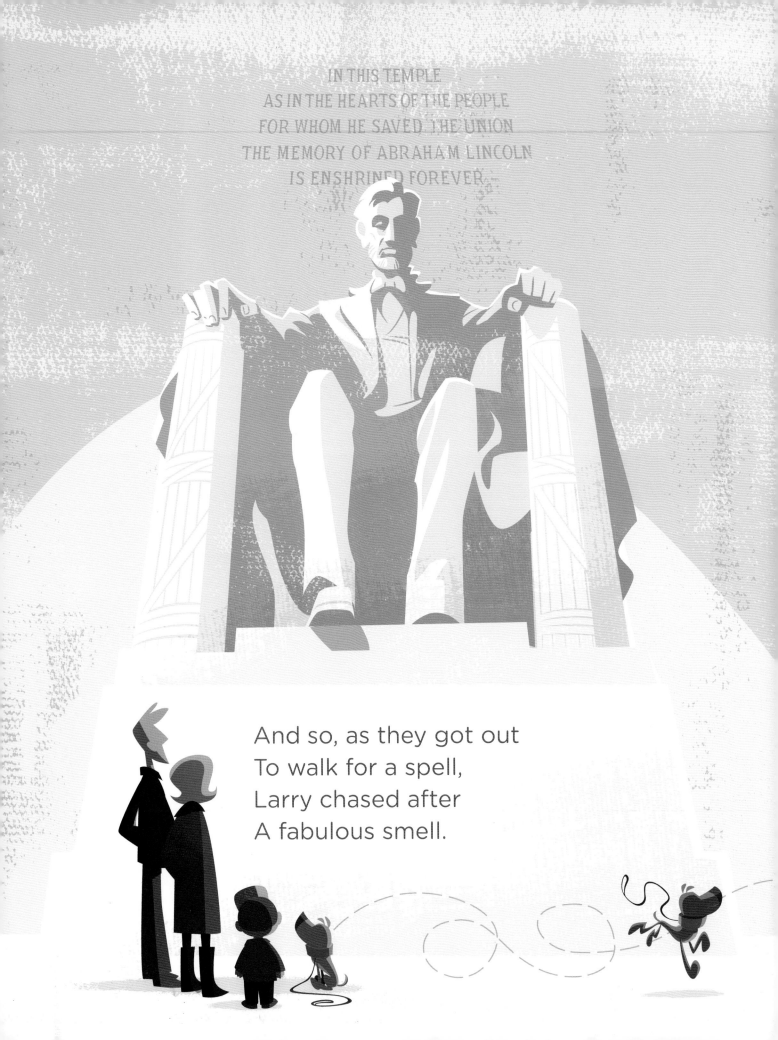

IN THIS TEMPLE
AS IN THE HEARTS OF THE PEOPLE
FOR WHOM HE SAVED THE UNION
THE MEMORY OF ABRAHAM LINCOLN
IS ENSHRINED FOREVER.

And so, as they got out
To walk for a spell,
Larry chased after
A fabulous smell.

LINCOLN MEMORIAL
This memorial was dedicated in 1922 to honor Abraham Lincoln, the sixteenth president of the United States. Lincoln was killed by John Wilkes Booth in Ford's Theatre on April 14, 1865, at the end of the Civil War.

He slurped and he chomped
The treat that he found
But when he looked up . . .

U.S. PARK POLICE

Haverstraw King's Daughters
Public Library

WASHINGTON MONUMENT

This monument was completed in 1884 to commemorate George Washington, commander of the Continental Army and the first president of the United States. It was the world's tallest man-made structure until the Eiffel Tower in Paris, France, was completed in 1889. It is still the world's tallest all-stone structure, standing over 555 feet tall.

. . . . Pete was nowhere around!

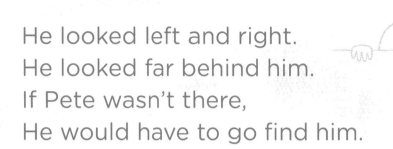

He looked left and right.
He looked far behind him.
If Pete wasn't there,
He would have to go find him.

Some men who might help him
Came into his view,
But they were just statues.
He'd look someplace new.

KOREAN WAR VETERANS MEMORIAL

WORLD WAR II MEMORIAL

THE WHITE HOUSE

Located at 1600 Pennsylvania Avenue NW, the White House has been the official residence of every US president since John Adams in 1800. The president is the head of the executive branch of the US government.

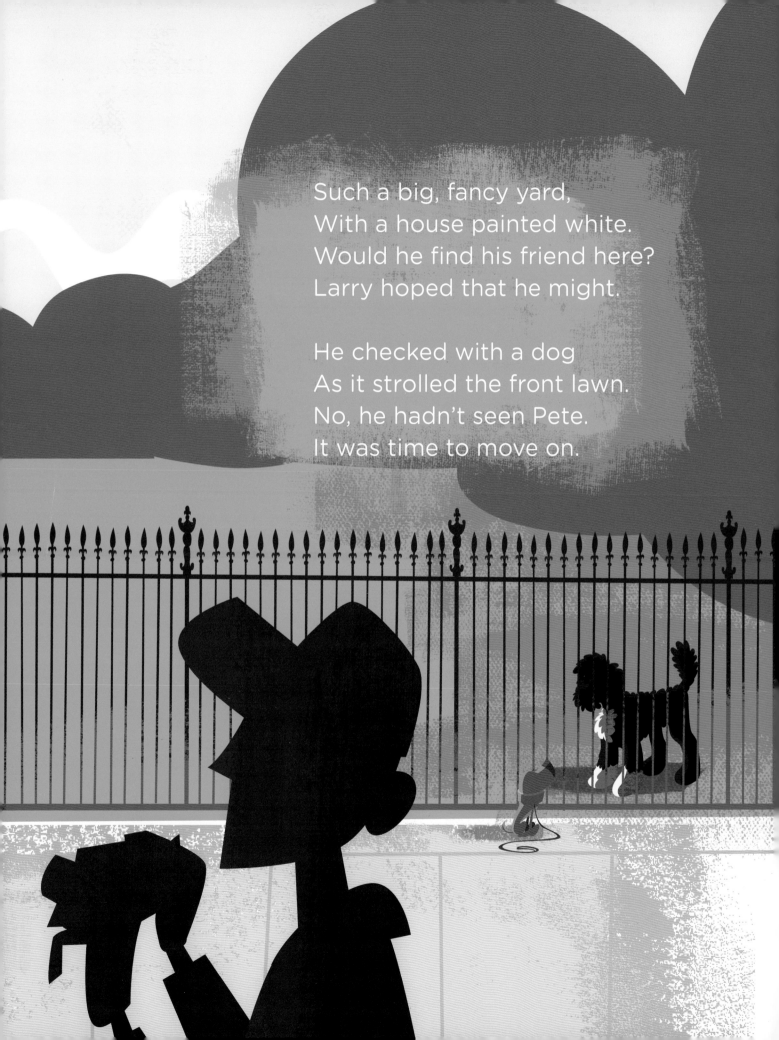

Such a big, fancy yard,
With a house painted white.
Would he find his friend here?
Larry hoped that he might.

He checked with a dog
As it strolled the front lawn.
No, he hadn't seen Pete.
It was time to move on.

NATIONAL ARCHIVES
BUILDING

NATIONAL MUSEUM OF
AMERICAN HISTORY

NATIONAL MUSEUM OF
NATURAL HISTORY

The
National Mall

WASHINGTON
MONUMENT

THE SMITHSONIAN
"CASTLE"

ARTS AND
INDUSTRIES
BUILDING

DEPARTMENT OF
AGRICULTURE

FREER
GALLERY
OF ART

ARTHUR M.
SACKLER
GALLERY

NATIONAL
MUSEUM OF
AFRICAN ART

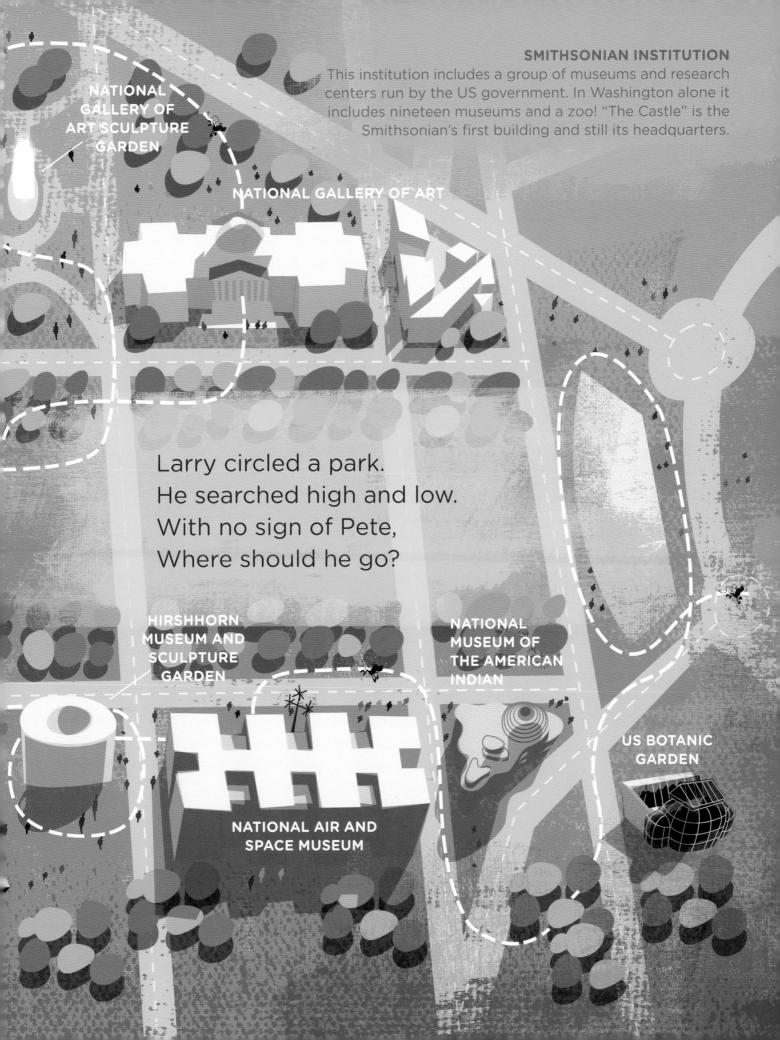

NATIONAL GALLERY OF ART SCULPTURE GARDEN

NATIONAL GALLERY OF ART

SMITHSONIAN INSTITUTION
This institution includes a group of museums and research centers run by the US government. In Washington alone it includes nineteen museums and a zoo! "The Castle" is the Smithsonian's first building and still its headquarters.

Larry circled a park.
He searched high and low.
With no sign of Pete,
Where should he go?

HIRSHHORN MUSEUM AND SCULPTURE GARDEN

NATIONAL MUSEUM OF THE AMERICAN INDIAN

US BOTANIC GARDEN

NATIONAL AIR AND SPACE MUSEUM

He ran up some steps
And then through a front door.
Had Pete gone inside?
Larry wasn't quite sure.

He saw whales and elephants,
Beasts of all kind,
But not the *one* boy
Larry wanted to find!

NATIONAL MUSEUM OF NATURAL HISTORY

Opened in 1910, this is the most visited natural history museum in the world. It's free to visit and open 364 days a year. The museum has over 125 million specimens in its collection.

These papers looked special,
But what did they say?
With no time to wonder,
He went on his way.

NATIONAL ARCHIVES
The National Archives is home to the so-called Charters of Freedom: the Declaration of Independence, the US Constitution, and the Bill of Rights (the first ten amendments of the Constitution). The lights are kept very low to prevent light damage to the documents.

Airplanes and rockets
That soar through the sky.
Would Pete and his family
Be somewhere nearby?

NATIONAL AIR AND SPACE MUSEUM
The National Air and Space Museum is the most popular museum in the country, with about seven million visitors a year. It holds the largest collection of historic aircraft and spacecraft in the world, including objects from antique gliders to Saturn V rockets and moon landers.

NATIONAL MUSEUM OF AMERICAN HISTORY

With a collection of more than three million artifacts, the museum is the primary depository of American historical items in the areas of social, political, cultural, scientific, and military history.

GEORGE WASHINGTON'S UNIFORM

STEAM LOCOMOTIVE *JUPITER*

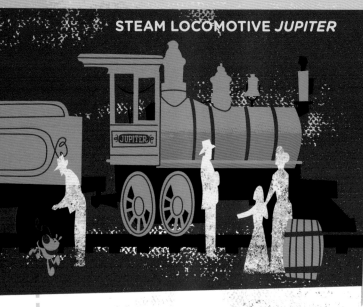

Larry stopped at a flag
Resting tattered and proud.
There were parents and kids
But no Pete in the crowd.

ABRAHAM LINCOLN'S HAT

DOROTHY'S RUBY SLIPPERS FROM *THE WIZARD OF OZ*

O! SAY CAN YOU SEE, BY THE DAWN'S EARLY LIGHT,
WHAT SO PROUDLY WE HAIL'D AT THE TWILIGHT'S LAST GLEAMING,
WHOSE BROAD STRIPES AND BRIGHT STARS THROUGH THE PERILOUS FIGHT
O'ER THE RAMPARTS WE WATCH'D, WERE SO GALLANTLY STREAMING?
AND THE ROCKETS' RED GLARE, THE BOMBS BURSTING IN AIR,
GAVE PROOF THROUGH THE NIGHT THAT OUR FLAG WAS STILL THERE;
O! SAY DOES THAT STAR-SPANGLED BANNER YET WAVE,
O'ER THE LAND OF THE FREE, AND THE HOME OF THE BRAVE?

THE STAR-SPANGLED BANNER
This flag flew over Fort McHenry
during the War of 1812, inspiring
Francis Scott Key to write the
lyrics to the national anthem.

He ran back outside
Where he spied a big dome.
Could this be where Larry
Would find his way home?

SENATE CHAMBER
There are one hundred US senators, two representing
each of the fifty states, each elected to a six-year term.
The vice president only votes in case of a tie.

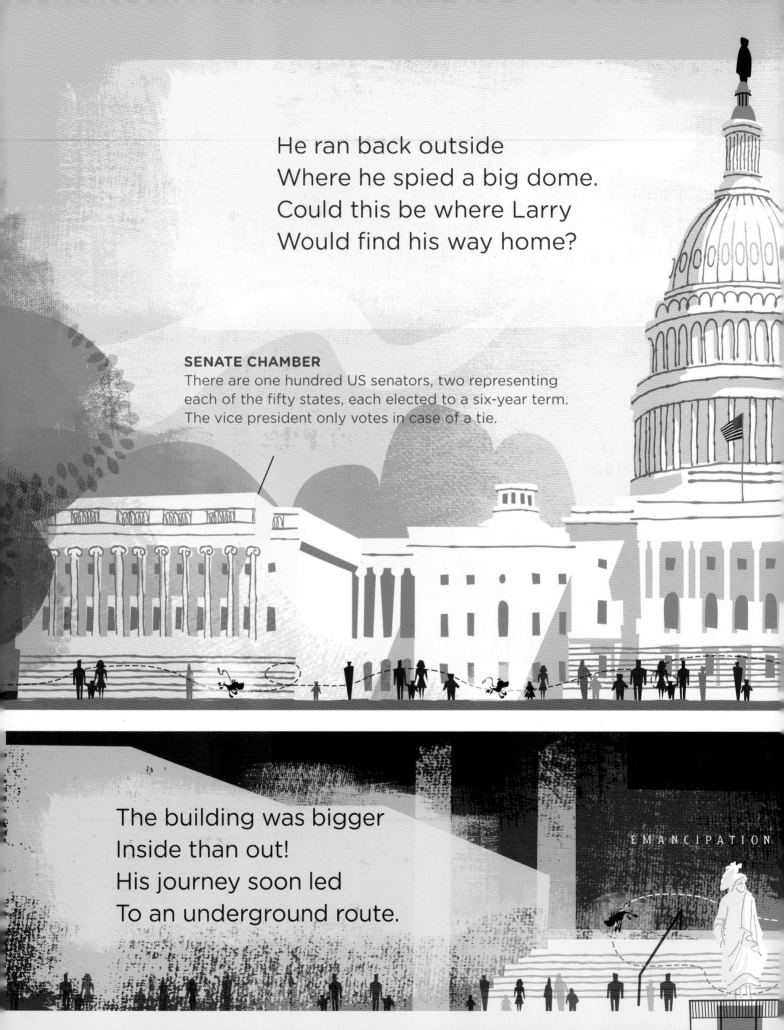

The building was bigger
Inside than out!
His journey soon led
To an underground route.

EMANCIPATION

US CAPITOL

This is the meeting place of the US Congress, which includes two houses, the Senate and the House of Representatives. Construction began in 1793, with a cornerstone laid by George Washington. Since then, the building has been expanded several times, and the dome was rebuilt after it burned down in the War of 1812. The Senate and the House make up the legislative branch of the US government.

HOUSE CHAMBER

There are 435 members of the House of Representatives, each serving a two-year term. The number of seats each state gets is determined by population: California has fifty-three seats, while seven states only have one: Alaska, Delaware, Montana, North Dakota, South Dakota, Vermont, and Wyoming.

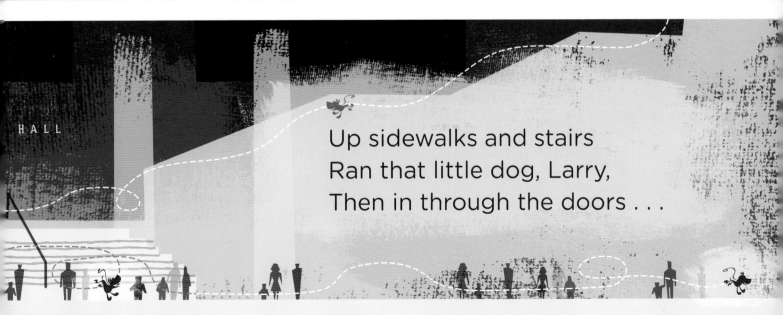

HALL

Up sidewalks and stairs
Ran that little dog, Larry,
Then in through the doors . . .

. . . to a giant library!

A dog wasn't welcome
In this quiet place.
They scolded and shushed him,
Then started to chase.

A pleasant librarian
Picked Larry up.
"Now, what shall we do
With this lost little pup?"

LIBRARY OF CONGRESS
The research library for the US Congress, founded in 1800, contains more than 23 million books. As the base of the US Copyright Office, all authors must submit two copies of every new book they write—including this one!

She took him outside
Where he wouldn't disturb,
And told him to "sit"
At the edge of the curb.

She looked at his collar
And pulled out her phone.
It seemed as if Larry
Would soon be back home.

MARTIN LUTHER KING JR. MEMORIAL
This memorial was opened in 2011 to honor the slain civil rights leader. The memorial's address, 1964 Independence Avenue SW, commemorates the Civil Rights Act of 1964, outlawing racial segregation.

The moment they heard the librarian's voice,
Pete and his parents began to rejoice.

SUPREME COURT OF THE UNITED STATES

The Supreme Court is composed of nine judges, called justices, each appointed to a lifetime term by the president. It is the highest court in the United States and the final interpreter of all federal law. The Supreme Court is the head of the judicial branch of the US government.

The boy and his dog
Couldn't be more delighted.
At last Pete and Larry
Had been reunited.

THOMAS JEFFERSON MEMORIAL
Completed in 1943, with the bronze
statue added in 1947, this memorial
commemorates Thomas Jefferson:
American Founding Father, primary
author of the Declaration of
Independence, and third president
of the United States.

They fell fast asleep
As their car drove away.
It had been an exciting,
Adventurous day!

Get More Out of This Book

Honoring the Past

Larry sees many monuments in Washington, DC, that honor events and people. Why is it important to have monuments for things that happened in the past? Can readers name monuments in their town? How many have visited the monuments mentioned in the book? Have they studied George Washington, Abraham Lincoln, and Martin Luther King Jr? Can they describe each one's influence on US History?

A Monster Library!

When Larry visits the Library of Congress, a librarian helps him get reunited with Pete. Explain to readers the purpose of the LOC. Discuss what kinds of activities readers have participated in at their local library. Would they like to find the other Larry Gets Lost books there? Would they like to someday write or illustrate their own book?

The Most Famous Address in America

When Larry wanders by the White House, he meets another dog. Do students know who the dog is? Who he belongs to? Ask readers to write a mock interview, having Larry ask questions about a dog's life in the White House.

One, Two, Three Branches of Government

Turn this page to see an illustration of the three branches of government. Can readers find and identify the corresponding pages/buildings in the book, locating the White House, the Supreme Court, and Congress? Do they feel that one branch is more important than the others? Do they think it's necessary to do this important work in a majestic building, or would a regular office building do? Why or why not?

TEACHER'S GUIDE: The above discussion questions and activities are from our teacher's guide, which is aligned to the Common Core State Standards for English Language Arts for Grades K to 1. For the complete guide and a list of the exact standards it aligns with, visit our website: SasquatchBooks.com

The Three Branches of Government

The President

EXECUTIVE BRANCH
Enforces Law

The Supreme Court

JUDICIAL BRANCH
Interprets Law

Congress

Senate

House of
Representatives

LEGESLATIVE BRANCH
Writes Law